This Little Tiger
book belongs to:

_____

_____

_____

For Benjamin, with love
~ M C B

To my daughter, Lara Macnaughton Bahrani
~ T M

LITTLE TIGER PRESS LTD,
an imprint of the Little Tiger Group
1 Coda Studios, 189 Munster Road, London SW6 6AW
www.littletiger.co.uk

First published in Great Britain 2018
This edition published 2019
Text copyright © M Christina Butler 2018
Illustrations copyright © Tina Macnaughton 2018

M Christina Butler and Tina Macnaughton have asserted
their rights to be identified as the author and illustrator of this
work under the Copyright, Designs and Patents Act, 1988

One Perfect Day

M Christina Butler • Tina Macnaughton

LITTLE TIGER
LONDON

It was a bright, breezy spring day
and Little Hedgehog and his friends
were going for a walk.

"What a perfect day!" smiled
Little Hedgehog, pulling on his hat.
"Let's see how many new flowers and
baby animals we can spot!"

"What a good idea!" cheered Badger.
And off they raced.

"Oh look!" Fox exclaimed,
peeping up into a tree.
"I can see baby birds!"

"And I've found the first
sweet violets!" said Rabbit.
"They're so beautiful!"

"There are fluffy white lambs
over here!" cried Little Hedgehog,
squeezing through the prickly hedge.
But then, "Oh dear!" he puffed.
"Now I'm stuck!"

With a big heave-ho,
Fox and Rabbit pulled
Little Hedgehog free.
"Wait!" he gasped.
"My hat's still stuck!"

"Don't worry, here it is!" smiled
Badger, untangling the hat
and popping it back on
Little Hedgehog's head.
   "Oh thank you!" beamed
Little Hedgehog.

Then something in the grass caught his eye.

"It's a chocolate egg," he cried. "Who's having an Easter egg hunt?"

"We are!" squeaked the baby mice. "Mummy Mouse planned it and you've found the first one!"

"You can have it," said Little Hedgehog, kindly.

"How fun!" said Rabbit. "I wonder where the eggs could be hidden." And the friends started to hunt high and low.

"Here!" squeaked the baby mice, scampering out of the long grass. "We've found one!"

"Well done!" smiled Little Hedgehog.

Suddenly, Mouse cried, "Listen! Can you hear that *cheep-cheep* noise?"

"I know what that is!" declared Badger. "Follow me."

Up ahead, five fluffy ducklings were darting in and out of the grass.

"Ooh!" exclaimed the friends.

"They look like yellow pompoms!" giggled Rabbit.

"What a lovely surprise!" chuckled Little Hedgehog.

"Hello," quacked Mother Duck. "We're supposed to be going for a swim but my little ones keep getting distracted. I'll never get them to the river at this rate!"

"We'll help!" offered Little Hedgehog. "We can look for eggs on the way."

With the friends keeping the ducklings
in line, they soon reached the river.
"I've found another egg!" squeaked
Mouse from amongst the flowers.

"Nearly there," called
Mother Duck. "Watch
your step!"
When the ducklings
saw the water, they waddled
towards it at once. All except
two, who darted off into
the long grass and away
from the river.

"Stop!" shouted Badger. "You're going
the wrong way!"

"Oh dear!" sighed Mother Duck.
"Where have they got to now?"

"Don't worry, we'll find them!" said
Little Hedgehog. "This way!"

And they all raced after the
ducklings into the wood.

The friends climbed over logs,
and hunted through the bushes.
As Rabbit peered under the
brambles he found another egg,
but no ducklings!

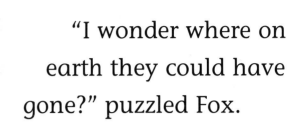

"I wonder where on
earth they could have
gone?" puzzled Fox.

Suddenly a baby mouse
called out, "Hurry up!
They're over here!"
They rushed after the
baby mice, scrambling
past bushes and trees . . .

. . . but when they caught up the ducklings were nowhere to be seen.

"You said you saw them!" grumbled Fox.

"They're definitely not here now!" sniffed Rabbit crossly.

"It's not our fault," piped up a baby mouse.
"You were too slow."

"Let's not get hot and bothered!" said
Little Hedgehog. "Listen – can you hear
that cheeping?"

Everyone followed the sound until they found,
sitting in the long grass, one of the little
lost ducklings!

"There you are!" Little Hedgehog chuckled,
scooping the duckling into his hat. "You'll
be safe and cosy in here."

"Thank you!" quacked Mother Duck,
racing up. "But how can I keep my
ducklings safe while we look for
their brother?"

"They can snuggle up in my hat!" offered
Little Hedgehog.
And so the search began again.
"I've found another egg!" called Fox.
"Me too!" cried Badger. "But no duckling!"

The friends hunted high and low, but they couldn't find the last little duckling anywhere!

Just then, as Little Hedgehog searched along the river bank, he discovered something wonderful.

"Come quickly!" he cried. "Look what I've found!"

There, nestled in the long grass, were the last three Easter eggs. And snuggled fast asleep with them was the little lost duckling!

"Hurrah!" quacked Mother Duck. "You've found him!"

"And all the eggs!" cheered the baby mice.

"Happy Easter!" Little Hedgehog beamed. "What a perfect end to a perfect day!"

MALPAS 5/7/19

More wonderful woodland tales from Little Tiger Press!

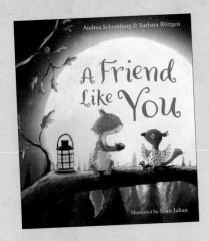

Andrea Schomburg & Barbara Röttgen

A Friend Like You

Illustrated by Sean Julian

SUZANNE CHIEW   CAROLINE PEDLER

BADGER AND THE Great JOURNEY

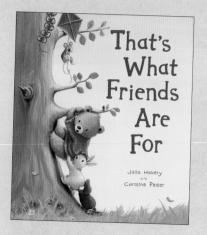

That's What Friends Are For

Julia Hubery
Caroline Pedler

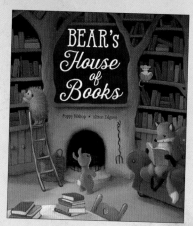

BEAR's House of Books

Poppy Bishop • Alison Edgson

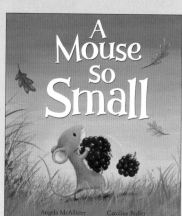

A Mouse So Small

Angela McAllister   Caroline Pedler

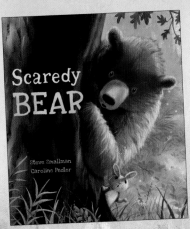

Scaredy BEAR

Steve Smallman
Caroline Pedler

For information regarding any of the above titles or for our catalogue, please contact us:
Little Tiger Press Ltd, 1 Coda Studios, 189 Munster Road, London SW6 6AW
Tel: 020 7385 6333 • E-mail: contact@littletiger.co.uk • www.littletiger.co.uk